To Mummy, Pitteli, Giovanni,
Alazar, and Henok A.L.

Text by Mary Joslin
Illustrations copyright © 2011 Anna Luraschi
This edition copyright © 2011 Lion Hudson

The moral rights of the author and illustrator
have been asserted

A Lion Children's Book
an imprint of
Lion Hudson plc
Wilkinson House, Jordan Hill Road,
Oxford OX2 8DR, England
www.lionhudson.com
Paperback ISBN 978 0 7459 6054 8
US Hardback ISBN 978 0 7459 6058 6

First paperback edition 2011
1 3 5 7 9 10 8 6 4 2 0
First US hardback edition 2012
1 3 5 7 9 10 8 6 4 2 0

A catalogue record for this book is available
from the British Library

Typeset in 16/22 ITC Esprit
Printed in China December 2011 (manufacturer LH17)

Distributed by:
UK: Marston Book Services Ltd, PO Box 269, Abingdon, Oxon OX14 4YN
USA: Trafalgar Square Publishing, 814 N Franklin Street, Chicago, IL 60610
USA Christian Market: Kregel Publications, PO Box 2607, Grand Rapids, MI 49501

SIMON AND THE EASTER MIRACLE

Mary Joslin

Illustrated by Anna Luraschi

LION
CHILDREN'S

Long ago, a farmer named Simon was making
his way to market.
   On his back he carried a pack of produce from
his farm. The weight made him stoop a little.
   He held a stout stick in his right hand to help
him keep his balance.
   In his left arm he cradled a basket of eggs.

Simon entered the city and plodded along the crowded streets.

"It's extremely busy for market day," he grumbled.
Then he remembered: it was a festival day too.

"Good – there will be more people who want to buy," he said.

As he turned a corner, he met an angry throng. The farmer watched in dismay.

Sneering soldiers were driving some weary wretch towards the city gate.

All around, people were jeering: "Crucify him, crucify him."

Simon stood back. He didn't want to get mixed up in any sort of trouble.

As the farmer watched, the prisoner fell under the weight of his own cross.

"Get up," barked the soldiers, and they goaded him with their swords. "Pick up that lump of wood and move."

But the man already bore the marks of a cruel beating they must have given him, and he could barely stand alone.

The officer looked round and saw the farmer with his pack.

"You!" he said. "You're strong. Get rid of that stuff
on your back and come and carry this cross."

There was no arguing. The officer's glinting sword made that perfectly clear.

Simon tucked his basket of eggs into a corner and leaned his pack and stick across to protect them.

Then he went to pick up the prisoner's cross, simply because he had to.

"Thank you," said the man to Simon. "I am grateful for your kindness."

The man's voice was gentle and his smile was sincere.

Simon was surprised. "What are you supposed to have done to deserve to die?" he asked.

The man shrugged slightly. "Preaching a message of peace," he said.

Together they reached the place of crucifixion: a rocky
hill just beyond the city walls.
Simon hurried away. He didn't want to hear the jeering
of the man's enemies.

Nor could he bear to hear the weeping of his friends.
"All I wished for today was a good market, with fair
prices for my produce," he said to himself.

W hen he reached the place where he had left his goods, he was dismayed.

The backpack had been overturned. His load of bread had been trampled.

His pitcher of wine had been spilt.

Only a dozen eggs were still whole, and even they were dirty and spattered.

"I may as well go home," said Simon. "Most of my produce is ruined. The best of the day has gone. It's not worth me setting up a stall."

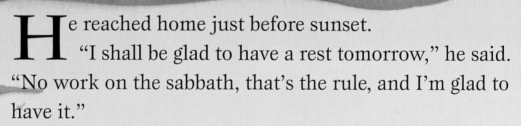

He reached home just before sunset.
"I shall be glad to have a rest tomorrow," he said.
"No work on the sabbath, that's the rule, and I'm glad to
have it."

He put the basket of eggs in his shed and sighed as he
locked the door.

It was early on Sunday morning when Simon went back.
 "What's this?" he said as he peered into his basket.
"The eggs are… empty. They weren't eggs for hatching."
 He was still puzzling about this as he fetched his pruning
knife and his sickle.

Then, as he worked in his olive grove, he heard the
sound of wings.
Twelve pure white doves came and flew around his head.
At once Simon knew that a miracle had happened.

"Doves are the birds of peace," he said. "And God blesses
all those who work for peace."
Simon watched the doves fly off beyond the far horizon.

And when he returned to his work, he noticed how quickly spring had warmed the new season's crops.